A Symphony of Our Stories

An Anthology

Massillon Public Library's Writers of the Round Table

Edited by Dawn E. Dagger, 2026.

You can find more information about this anthology at: queenanneslacepublishing.com.

Foreword

The Massillon Public Library Adult Writer's Group was established in February of 2023. It was only supposed to last the month of February, to help kickstart writers' passion and to kick off the Your Novel is Now multi-month program at the library.

However, the writing group was such a success that it lasted far beyond February. In February of 2024, they deemed themselves the "Writers of the Round Table."

Many of the writers have since released their own books, and their writing careers have grown far beyond their dreams.

The group meets twice a month, and has supported authors with editing, formatting, proofreading, and—most importantly—encouragement.

You can learn more about the Writers of the Round Table or join us by visiting: massillonlibrary.org

Also by the Writers of the Round Table

Writing Is: A Poetry Collection

Olio: A Short Story Anthology

Dandelions in Sidewalk Cracks: A Poetry Collection

Contents

WOODWINDS: SAMPLING

Dwight Parrish

WHEN STRUNG OUT ON the Funk
Beethoven set me free
Then came Bach
Then came Brahms...
with Symphony #3

The first and second chair
for Flutes and Clarinets
I saw the sound
I saw the chords
with notes I can't forget

I waltzed into a trance

thru softness and thru loud
The Double Bass
The Celtic Harp
were drifting on a cloud

They took me for a ride
so very far away
The Tuba's burp
The Trombone's vibe
forced all my nerves to sway

Well...

Bach can toot a French Horn
That Brahms knows how to jam
But Ludwig sneaks
into the groove
My heart and soul goes "Damn!"

HARMONICA: My Father's Secret

Cat Russell

ALL PARENTS KEEP SECRETS from their children.

Aside from gifts at Christmas or surprise parties, this fact had never occurred to me. At least, not *my* parents. They had never had lives of their own before I sprung, unbidden, from the foot of my mother's hospital bed. And don't try to argue me out of this vision: the alternative is something I simply won't contemplate.

Obviously, they had never been people before I was born. I suspect all children see their parents this way. They were never young, never snuck cookies before dinner, nor held hobbies or dreams of their own. How could they? They weren't fully formed until their lives belonged to their children. To us. To me.

My mother stayed home to cook and clean before bills forced her to take a job at a local bank, while my father worked within biking distance. He'd grown his business from almost nothing, yet it sustained my family throughout my childhood. He went to work and came home at the same time every day, always arriving just minutes before dinner was on the table. My parents went out every week to Kiwanis or Elks or Knights of Columbus, dancing as they had when they first met years before I was born.

So you see, despite growing up in the '80s when MTV, feathered hair, and Rubik's Cubes abounded, I grew up in a black-and-white world of '50s sitcoms with older parents. They married and had me in their late thirties, so by my standards, they were ancient. Way too old to harbor secrets.

Occasionally my father would do something wildly creative that impressed the hell out of me. He created a character called *Brother Charles* that performed at the Knights of Columbus with a bottle of "Brother Charles's Miracle Tonic" that bore a suspicious resemblance to a whiskey bottle; it was hysterical! Another time, he took an art class, and I was mesmerized by the charcoal sketches within his spiral bound assignment book.

But I never suspected this.

Harmonicas.

Not a single harmonica. I never noticed one in our home, never heard him play, at any point in the nearly two decades I lived with them.

My most vivid musical memory of him during my formative years was when he hummed and swayed to country music blaring on the cheap radio in his shop. Once, I danced with him at a concert at a local rodeo arena, kicking up the sawdust floor beneath the hot Florida sun.

But I don't remember a single harmonica.

Nor do I remember, at any point in my childhood, seeing the multitude that greeted me when I returned home to visit as a newly married adult. I'd been gone a while, and he had converted my old room into his private music studio. The closet that had once held my clothes was now stuffed with the discarded remnants of my childhood: my old dollhouse, the tiny cabinet my grandfather had built, my mother's old porcelain dolls, and a large wooden case my father pulled out with pride. He couldn't wait to show me his prize.

Inside the heavy case, fitted into molded compartments lined in sumptuous blue velvet, were his treasures: his harmonicas.

I had never seen so many in one place in my entire life.

Now, granted, I had not lived that long, but none of my previous experience had prepared me for that. The instruments were of varying sizes: the largest the size of a brick and the smallest tiny enough to fit on a chain.

He explained in detail how each made different types of sounds.

I stuttered uncontrollably for a full minute before I finally managed to ask when he learned to play.

"College!" He grinned that goofy dad grin I knew so well, as I wondered if I really knew him at all. "I used to play all the time, but I started engraving things on the side to make a little extra money, and then that took off..."

And I just then realized he meant the art college he attended while living in Mexico. Who was this stranger? He showed off his room—my former sanctuary—the amps and microphone and other equipment. I remember some weird pedal somewhere whose use was a complete mystery to me. Just like the man before me.

Years later, my father lay dying in a hospital bed in the room he'd shared with my mother for over four decades. As I sat beside him, I wondered how much of the person he had been I'd missed. Throughout my years away, I'd call every week but mostly spoke with my mother; he was always out doing things—mowing the yard, cleaning the pool, playing "gigs" with his harmonica group. I never knew there was such a thing as a harmonica-only group before the day he debuted that wooden case, but he regularly performed in one at local restaurants and clubs.

As he lay in that bed, looking nothing like the man I'd admired my whole life, his many friends stopped by at different times throughout the day to check on my mother or drop off small gifts. I clasped a photo in one shaking hand taken the week before he collapsed by the pool: my father playing his harmonica, surrounded by friends. I wondered what song it had been.

When my mother called, days earlier, to tell me he had fallen and did not have long to live, I flew with my husband and son many miles back to my childhood home. Except for the hospital bed in my parents' room, everything was as I remembered from my last visit—even the music room. I remembered how I'd resented his annexation of my childhood territory to his musical ambitions, despite the fact I hadn't lived there for years—and my cheeks burned with shame. Why had I never known how important it was to him?

Daydreaming memories of earlier times, I remembered how he had sung "Santa Claus is Coming to Town" to me, when I was a little girl, in an effort to stem my childish tears one Christmas season. I remembered the way he'd hum and sway his hips whenever Kenny Rogers or the Oakridge Boys came on the radio. I remembered the way he twirled my mother as they danced to a cover of Eric Clapton's "Cocaine" at Hemingway's famous hangout in Key West.

He'd lived abroad, painted murals, sketched in charcoal that stained my fingers as I turned each page of his sketchbook. I'd seen black-and-white pictures of him as a young man wearing white t-shirts with a pack of cigarettes rolled up in the sleeve. He'd been young once. As young as me, and younger still. Why had I never bothered to find out more of who he was before he became the man I knew and loved, the father who played chess with me despite my taking twenty minutes to make each move?

And he didn't let me win. He played patiently, knowing I needed to earn each victory—no matter how long I took to accomplish it.

After a week's vigil by my dying father's side, I was forced to return home to Ohio, where days later I received the call. My father had passed. I remember answering my cell as I sat in bed next to my husband. I remember hanging up. I remember arms around me.

In the days that followed, my mind drifted back. The money from the sold house would help pay for my mother's care and expenses at her new residence. That was something, at least, though I wished she could stay in the home she'd known my entire life. The hospice nurses that tended my father in his final days assured me she needed extra care and should not live on her own. How would she deal with her loneliness? At least her new place was set up to be social, with communal dining, games, movies, and other group activities. She'd need to be around other people.

I returned to Florida over a weekend for the funeral and to help my mother empty the house for a new family. She watched the accumulated wealth of her life packed up in neat brown boxes, donated, or—worst of all—set out on the curb to be taken as trash, if not taken by strangers.

It was Hell.

The funeral had been arranged ahead of time, so we only needed to show up. The funeral director liked my dad and sent a complimentary limo to bring us to and from the funeral home—the only time in my life I've ever been in such an extravagant vehicle. We went to the service, and when I saw my father laying there, I knew he was really gone. The shell that remained wasn't him. It looked nothing like him, except in the most superficial sense: brown hair, two arms, two hands clasped across his front. I couldn't see his eyes, but didn't need to see them to know he was well and truly gone.

And yet, the room was packed, brimming with life. People milled throughout the large space, and many filed in front of us to grasp each of our hands and wish us well or share some anecdote about my father. I told my mother, "Dad would have appreciated that his funeral is on April Fool's Day, because he was such a joker." She heartily agreed, and even chuckled sadly at the obvious truth. Someone so full of life, who constantly joked and laughed often, would have found the date entirely appropriate. And though we were mostly numb, when we returned home to the home that wasn't anymore, there was comfort in knowing he was missed by more than just ourselves. He had been well and truly loved.

That weekend, I had little room in my travel bag for mementos to bring back to Ohio, but I made sure to take two things: one, the bathrobe he loved that still smelled like his cologne, and two, his no-frills everyday harmonica. The one he would wear in the pocket of his button-down shirt.

When I finally arrived home, I cocooned myself in the folds of his maroon-colored robe, enveloped in his scent, and tried (unsuccessfully) to blow a perfect, clear note with his harmonica, knowing the last breath that passed through it had been his.

CYMBALS: Obsession

John Echols

He had long loved the cymbals.

He hadn't known or understood why, but he couldn't deny his obsession with the huge, metallic instruments. The love had started when he was a youth. Something about the cymbals drew him from the first time he'd heard them. They represented power, they were somewhat intimidating. The cymbals spoke with a voice of their own.

His parents had told him often that he always sat at attention when he heard the cymbals, even in grade school. His parents had even bought him some small, plastic toy cymbals from a dollar store to keep him occupied for periods of time. But, Paul Francis soon discovered those cymbals didn't make any sound, so he quickly lost interest.

The sound made the instrument, Paul thought. What good were quiet cymbals? He didn't see the point. Couldn't his parents find one that had some kind of recording of actual cymbal music? But, the plastic ones were still cymbals, so he'd kept them around, if for no other reason than they were a persistent reminder of where it all started.

When he got old enough to join the high school marching band, his choice of instrument was easy. The cymbals sat there; inviting him, beckoning him, almost calling him. He couldn't refuse. He was under their spell. It was as if the cymbals knew his name and used it to draw him.

He'd represented the North High School Marching Band well for four years, with his trusty cymbals accompanying him. The cymbals made him feel important, almost godlike. It was as if the cymbals were nothing more than an extension of his arms. They felt natural, like they were just supposed to be there. He'd learned to play them so fast and so well he rarely had to even practice. Everything about them seemed automatic to Paul. His girlfriend, Trish, had taken to calling him "the Natural" for his musical gifts.

Paul had often wondered why his interest was so great in the cymbals. He had no explanation. He wondered if it was a genetic thing. Neither of his parents had ever indicated any musical interest at all, with cymbals or any other instrument. Paul wondered if they had heard any cymbals when his mom discovered she was pregnant with him.

Oh well, he thought. *It had to come from somewhere.* And even if he'd never know where, his interest wasn't going away. Obviously. So, he would just have to accept it. And so would everyone else.

One thought always remained with him. The cymbals were him and he was the cymbals. Period. End of story. He would entertain no debate about it and no thoughts of changing his perspective. He recalled times if he wondered seriously if he valued the cymbals above Trish. She had wondered too. Audibly.

In college, Paul continued in the band with his trusty cymbals flanking him. He'd been able to travel all over the country with his college band, showcasing his prized cymbals for the whole nation to see. They were his children now, those cymbals. He laughed, remembering asking himself if he should name them. He'd gone as far as considering Chang and Eng as the names of his cymbals. Romulus and Remus had been another consideration. But, that was ridiculous, wasn't it? He wondered...

Eventually, college ended and, with it, Paul's band career. He moped about it, wondering where to go from there. Wherever he went, his cymbals, apparently, weren't going with him. It would be like parting ways with a dear friend, or breaking up with someone you thought was your soulmate. It was not going to be a smooth breakup, but he steeled his resolve and did it.

Life had to go on. Reality had to set in. He'd have to get a job, a home. Those thoughts made him cringe. Doing these things without his cymbals made it an even more daunting task.

But, did his cymbals really have to depart from him? Really? What harm would it do to keep them around? They weren't going to hurt anything or anyone. So, his mind was made up. It hadn't been much of a battle, though. All Paul needed was any reason not to part with his prized cymbals. He couldn't take them to work, but they could stay at his home while he worked.

Paul soon got employment as an orderly in the local hospital. He loved his work, he loved the people. He loved the interactions. And it paid well. Soon, Paul wondered if he could bring his cymbals to work, at least as entertainment for the patients. That plan was shut down by the head nurse, Hilda. The old woman with the German accent said cymbals would "disrupt" the operations of the hospital and the peace thereof. Translation: cymbals would be much too loud for the hospital. Paul sighed resignedly upon receiving the news.

As time went on, Paul found less and less time for his cymbals. They sat there in his two-bedroom home, just staring at him; imploring him, beckoning him, making their case to be back in his life.

Trish, Paul's once and again girlfriend, had suggested he sell them. Paul was appalled by the suggestion. He thought Trish understood. He was shocked she would even suggest such a thing. The mere thought of treating his beloved cymbals as nothing more than merchandise was cringe-inducing, almost insulting. The resulting argument would always end with Trish just shaking her head and leaving Paul alone with his cymbals. Paul wondered if Trish felt threatened by them. But that was silly. Wasn't it?

"Nah," Paul told himself, "Trish is more mature than that."

Sleep was uneasy that night.

Trish was loyal, at least somewhat, as long as she was interested. She'd left Paul before, for some reason long forgotten. She had come back, though, for a bit before leaving again. He cast a knowing eye in the direction of the cymbals. They had never left him. Ever. For any reason. They stayed with him, faithfully. They remained silent, caused no issues, and took up little space. Sometimes, he wondered which side he would fall on if he ever had to make a choice between Trish and the cymbals. The cymbals had been his lifelong friends. Trish, well, not so much.

Life went on, even for Paul. He attended both his parents' funerals, both times struggling to leave his cymbals at home. The clash of the cymbals still played in his head during the services. He could almost feel the vibrations of it, clanging after every point the preacher emphasized in his eulogy. Even after the services, Paul found it hard to grieve for his parents. After all, he still had his cymbals.

Paul begun to settle in at home with Trish. Somewhat. He found simple tasks difficult. His thoughts kept wandering to those cymbals, sitting alone and abandoned in the extra room. He couldn't play at home, since the noise annoyed Trish. There was really no place to play them in town. Sometimes, Paul would just sit and stare at them for long stretches of time. He still couldn't get rid of them. They were part of him, like a significant other. Trish would just have to get over it.

Life passed. Paul and Trish had a good relationship. Things went well. Paul was quite happy with Trish. He almost wanted to say that 'L' word, he'd avoided saying for many years. Strangely, he couldn't force himself to say it without looking warily at his cymbals, as if waiting for their approval. He wanted to say it, but he just couldn't force himself to do it. The words wouldn't come. His mouth wouldn't cooperate.

Paul laughed uneasily the times that Trish suggested he should marry his cymbals. He didn't know if she was joking or not. He also didn't know what his response would be should that scenario ever unfold. He smiled at the thought. But was he thinking about Trish as he smiled or was he thinking about the cymbals? He wasn't sure.

He knew his obsession with the cymbals was kinda weird, but everybody had some kink in their lives, right? He'd tried, unsuccessfully, to deal with his, uh, situation, before. Nothing worked. Paul concluded he was just meant to be with the cymbals. There would be no argument about it. God, he told himself, wanted it this way.

Middle age came and not much changed for Paul. He'd go to work and spend his shift with the cymbals in the back of his mind. He'd sit through meetings, wondering when the meeting would end. His cymbals awaited him.

His coworkers considered him weird. They didn't really know him, but they'd heard the stories. They tended to just walk by him and smile or look at him strangely. It was okay, though. Trish often did the same things. Still. If he could deal with Trish, he could deal with his coworkers, even Steve and Nancy from HR. They had both, at separate times, tried to convince Paul to donate his cymbals for one of the giveaways his companies did during the summer. He'd laughed those propositions off. Why should someone else have his cymbals? They were his, right? And the thought of him handing them off to someone else was insulting, even to his cymbals. And for a "good cause"? Paul, himself, was the best cause he could think of.

As he grew older and retirement came ever closer, Paul still kept his cymbals close at hand. He hadn't played them in some time, but he'd practiced, much to Trish's chagrin. Paul had kept the cymbals polished and clean, faithfully tending to them weekly. Trish had stayed beside him all these years, despite the cymbals. She had been loyal for at least ten years. He really loved her and appreciated her. She had, apparently, accepted his relationship with his instruments.

Although he'd stopped actively playing the cymbals, Paul could still hear them clanging musically and methodically in his head. They comforted him, even in their physical absence. They brought him peace and encouragement. No matter what the situation, the cymbals were always there for him. Always.

Trish and Paul never married, although they stayed together as a couple until they reached senior citizenship. Their union hadn't produced any children, but Paul always thought of his cymbals as his partner and cherished them like his children. Trish wasn't going to go that far. Paul often wondered what was wrong with her.

As it turned out, however, what was wrong with Trish was scleroderma. She had suffered joint pain and issues with cold weather for years. She had been diagnosed years earlier, but she just dealt with it, as was her nature. She struggled mightily, but she just plugged along. He had asked repeatedly if she wanted a cymbal symphony. She'd always responded with a dirty look but a sly smile.

This time was different. This time Trish was dying. The disease had taken its toll. Even as she lay in her hospital bed, Paul still felt drawn to his cymbals which sat at home. His mind kept wandering back there. Since Trish was being treated at the same hospital that had already banned his cymbals, there was little chance he could bring them back there. He fidgeted nervously, hoping Trish would be released... if for no other reason than he could then get back to his cymbals.

But Trish would not be released. Not this time. She finally succumbed to scleroderma on April 1st.

"Some April Fools Day surprise," he muttered to himself. Something was taken from Paul's soul that day. It hurt. But he still had his cymbals. Everything would be alright now, right? His excitement somewhat muted, Paul headed home.

Even with his trusty cymbals there to accompany him, Paul found the grieving process difficult.

The cymbals didn't dry his tears. They didn't cure the hole in his heart. They didn't fix the problem. Not that Paul didn't give them the chance. But when he went to his cymbals with tears in his eyes, the cymbals just sat there, mute and unfeeling. He couldn't make the cymbals understand.

It had been ten years since Trish left him. Paul still missed her. His cymbals remained, but now, Paul regarded them differently. He often wondered what their purpose had really been in his life. He often pondered the things he missed out on because he was more concerned about his cymbals. Why had he allowed two inanimate objects to become his main focus in life? Those thoughts just brought him back to Trish.

Now, at age seventy-seven, alone and regretful, Paul looked upon the cymbals as never before. After some deep thought, the light bulb finally came on in Paul's mind. The cymbals he'd heard in his head were just that, *symbols.*

He'd heard them whenever a major life event was upon him. He'd heard them, in his mind, before the deaths of both his parents. He'd heard them mere hours before Trish died. That was it.

Now, Paul faced his own mortality. His health had been declining for years, exacerbated by the loss of Trish. Actually, since his parents' deaths, his health had been a concern. Trish had tried to get him to get regular checkups, but Paul couldn't take his cymbals, so, he wasn't interested. Paul had been ready for his own demise, but not Trish's. She wasn't supposed to go first. She was the good one, the smart one, the kind, soft one. Now, there were no more tomorrows for them.

As he sat on a Thursday night, fighting his own physical issues, Paul heard the faint clash of the cymbals. Saturday, Paul noticed the clash getting louder. Daily, the volume increased. Paul considered going to the hospital, but why? He knew what the sound of the cymbals meant. Only this time, the cymbal wasn't clanging for his parents, or for Trish.

The cymbals clanged for him now. They were no longer a source of joy and cheer, but an omen, a harbinger, a herald.

Now, the cymbals Paul had enjoyed all his life were signaling the end of his life. He didn't know when, but

Paul knew the end was coming. Soon. Paul didn't know if he was ready, but he guessed, it didn't matter now. The curtain was closing on his life. The darkness was coming for him. Quickly. Soon.

Paul didn't panic. He leaned back in his favorite chair, thoughtful and wary. He accepted it. He almost chuckled at it. The cymbals had been there as his comfort. Now, they were there to usher him into the afterlife. The cymbals really had been there all his life, even at the end of it.

Paul wondered if his cymbals would be returned to him in Heaven. He'd rather have them than have a harp. But, what if he didn't make it to Heaven? What would become of his cymbals then? In Hell, would his cymbals be burned? Would they be replaced by an instrument like the oboe? Would he be forced to play the piano for eternity? The thought chilled him.

Paul awakened with a start early Sunday morning. He tried to adjust his eyes, but it was difficult. Even movement itself was difficult. Trish stood before him. But that was impossible.

Then he heard it. A low sound at first, slowly gaining in volume. Trish just smiled, her arms open. She was Trish again, before the disease, completely healthy. The musical score intensified behind her. Paul recognized the tune as the work of Buddy Rich in the Concert for the Americas. It didn't matter now, anyway.

As the crescendo grew, Paul found the strength to stand. He made his way over to Trish, who still remained in place, welcoming Paul into her arms.

They embraced, an embrace that Paul had missed for years. The crescendo grew. It could not be blocked out. Paul wondered if the neighbors would complain, but he didn't care. He knew what was coming.

The snuggle was just as Paul remembered. Warm, realistic, and enduring. Trish whispered, "It's time to come home, baby." She smiled broadly as she regarded him.

A mighty clash of the cymbals followed.

As Trish held his hand, Paul felt his life force slipping away. His will to stay in this world also waned. The cymbals sounded the crash note. He knew what that meant. He held onto Trish's hand more tightly and returned her dazzling smile.

Paul Francis passed from this life shortly after 7 a.m. on Sunday. He left with a smile on his face, in the arms of his beloved Trish. The cymbals played a funeral march as he died.

The cymbals had, indeed, been there for him until the end.

CELLO: Cello Steps

LML McClure

Chapter One

THE SOOTHING, QUIET STRAINS of the opening measures of Pachelbel's "Canon in D" awakened Leise. She hadn't heard the name of the cellist announced by the classical radio station, but it didn't matter. It was her favorite piece of music and, in her opinion, it was a perfect melody for waking up quietly when played on a cello.

"*Aging is not for the faint-hearted.*" Leise couldn't remember who first wrote or said that, but she often thought of that phrase when she was getting out of bed. Her knees really hurt that day, but she needed to get moving. She smiled, though, even as she groaned, at the irony of forgetting the source of the frequently-repeated phrase.

She should act her age and research the source as a good former teacher should.

It was fortunate for both her and the furry face staring at her that she had to feed the cat. It was both a basic, humane act and an emotional response. She really did like her current kitty. Since her retirement, there were many days when she would have stayed in bed much too late if not for the persistent, quiet meow every morning at six, her regular wakeup time for the past twenty-four years. The cat didn't need an alarm; she just knew it was the time Leise fed her, even if there was an incorrect hour on the clock during the seasonal time changes. Leise smiled again as she remembered all the jokes about pets refusing to accept the fact that Eastern Daylight Savings time had "fallen" back to Standard Time. It was "time to feed me!" no matter what that clock said.

The problem was she often lacked the self-discipline to stay up, or to at least obey her alarm set for eight-thirty. She usually hit the snooze or the stop button and slept another two hours, making breakfast a brunch many days. Fortunately, she could force herself out from under the blankets on Sundays and other days when she had an earlier appointment or commitment. She kept repeating to herself she had to develop a better "go to bed earlier" rule. It didn't help when friends or relatives said, "But you're retired! You don't have to get up early!" Yes, maybe, but she really didn't need to watch TV or read until midnight most evenings either.

Leise turned on the coffeemaker and then popped the lid on the cat food can (she did have priorities after all), trying to see if the kitchen wall calendar had any notes in the square for the day's date. She didn't see any writing in the Tuesday box. "Oh, rats!" It was Wednesday, wasn't it? That meant it was Silver Sneaker Better Balance and Chair Yoga Day at the Y. It would be a quick yogurt, toast, and banana breakfast instead of something more leisurely. An "only one cup of coffee" morning.

She would look forward to a stop at her favorite coffee shop after the exercise class. She could rationalize splurging with one of those chocolate muffins as she enjoyed her second cup of caffeine. After all, she had stretched her arms and legs and moved the sore knees first, right? Maybe later she could also play Pachelbel again and process to the cello's rhythm with extra leg stretching.

Chapter Two

Leise was focused on being thankful as she left the hospital. It was Thanksgiving Day, so it was easy to "think thanks." Fortunately, her cousin, Michelle, was feeling a bit better, and the cardiologist hoped her medical team could complete the heart catheterization on Friday. The doctors needed to know if her heart suffered any damage during her bout with severe pneumonia. Leise was keeping her schedule open so she could take Michelle home, hopefully soon.

As she left the hospital, Leise pushed the Yo-Yo Ma CD into her car player. She let the "Prélude of the Cello Suite N 1 in G Major" calm her. She was thankful she had a supportive family to depend on if she ever became so ill. Her brother had given the usual Thanksgiving dinner invitation to join him and her sister-in-law, and her sister who lived nearby would also be joining them. But Leise decided she would just go home. The weather was uncertain, and she didn't want to make the forty-minute drive home in the dark, especially if the rain/snow mix continued. She had already alerted her siblings she probably wouldn't come, and she confirmed in a quick text she would actually cook a bit for herself that evening. She was thankful she felt independent enough to be on her own. She was not feeling lonely, but rather felt their support and best wishes. They were glad she could be available for Michelle.

As she entered her apartment, she actively gave thanks again for the opportunity to live there. The rent was cheaper, the mid-room gave additional storage space as well as an office space, and she had a washer/dryer combo again. That luxury was missed when she had moved to the other senior apartment complex the prior year. While she was thankful for the nearby, clean laundromat in that city, she was not missing those trips now that she had been able to purchase the washer/dryer tower from the former tenant.

The only disadvantage was that the lint filter to the dryer was at the back. Leise was used to no longer being able to use the top cabinet shelves in the kitchen, but this was new. She no longer felt safe climbing on a stepladder or stepstool to reach the high places. So, the first few times she tried to pull out the dryer filter, she was a bit dismayed. She could *just* reach the lower finger hole to grab the filter as long as she had the extra inch provided by her sneakers. The first time she tried it while wearing her slippers, it was an utter failure and arm muscle strain experience.

She had almost perfected the correct angle to push the cleaned lint filter back in its slot at the back corner of the dryer. She often shouted in celebration if she got it in the first or second time.

Almost every time she pulled out and replaced the filter, she gave thanks for her sweet 6‘4“ brother who always helped her with the other “height-needed” jobs where she lived. Curtain rod installations, light bulb replacements, smoke alarm battery checks, and picture hanging were among the many gifts he had given her over the years. Leise was truly thankful for the blessing of her family.

She popped in her “Pachelbel’s Canon in D” CD to listen to more cello strains as she prepared her Thanksgiving meal.

Chapter Three

"And how are you tonight, Young Lady?"

Leise gave the man a strained smile and a "Fine, thank you." She had heard such a condescending greeting before, but she didn't want to correct the person with her true feelings. She was no longer young, but that didn't bother her. Her age had also given her a maturity in human interactions, she hoped. So, she didn't say aloud her thoughts: *You just lost a potential client, buddy, but I'm staying for the free dinner anyway!*

At least he hadn't addressed her as "Little Lady." She would have lost her maturity and been strongly tempted to say in her deepest voice, "Are you talking to me?"

She was attending a Medicare seminar sponsored by a well-known health insurance company. One of the co-sponsors was a new health care facility in the area, and together the presenters hoped to recruit new clients with their presentations after the free meal in a nice local restaurant. Leise had already decided she wasn't changing her primary care provider and the corresponding medical system, but she did want to change her Medicare health insurance plan. Hence, her attendance at the event. The free chicken sandwich was a bonus.

After an informative presentation by the insurance company representative, Leise talked briefly with the couple who were sharing her table. She realized that she had been blessed with her retirement income after they mentioned financial struggles due to poor health and the need to start Social Security earlier than recommended. The correct choice for their Medicare health plan was possibly more important than hers. She was thankful for the previous counsel she had received and multiple resources available for her review as she researched her current medical insurance company.

Leise planned to change to a different coverage that enrollment period and was waiting for an appointment with an insurance broker closer to her home. But the woman at the seminar was a good second lead if Leise didn't "click" with the other broker. She was also very respectful and knowledgeable. Leise enjoyed speaking with her and was glad to receive the broker's contact information.

The positive interaction at the end of the seminar made up for the irritating greeting at the door and the dry chicken sandwich. She was also disappointed in the lack of accommodations in the small restroom and the stairs to the banquet room. Shouldn't a seminar sponsor of a product catering to older adults be more aware of the access needs of possibly disabled clientele?

She probably should give the restaurant another chance, Leise thought as she walked to her car. Her previous managers had often had business meals at the location. However, she had developed a stronger shell in the last few years of her aging experience. This "young lady" was very willing to say *no* to businesses that were unwilling to accept her fully as an older customer. Lack of accommodations to this mature, older adult would mean Leise would take her business elsewhere. After all, she grinned, she was a tough "young lady.

As she quickened her steps to her car, she was humming the "A"llemande of the Cello Suite N 3 in C Major" from her Yo-Yo Ma CD.

Chapter Four

Leise had almost completed the mandatory ten hikes to receive her new hiking staff and the 2024 Park Challenge shield. Although she hadn't been able to complete the suggested round-trip mileage for each trail, she had walked one to two miles round trip for seven of the listed locations. She had started hike #8 too late in the afternoon, forgetting after the time change the sun set closer to five. That nice walk was only about a half-mile round trip. She wouldn't count that one unless she ran out of time to complete the challenge.

Leise had smiled when she saw a picture of the 2024 Challenge shield. It was a turtle holding a hiking staff. Leise had often called herself the "turtle sister" when compared to her two sisters, who had run half marathons. Friends and family always encouraged her with comments as "Yes, but you are walking!" or "Slow and steady wins the race, right?" She didn't have the leg strength to even jog very slowly anymore, nor could her knees handle uneven ground or steeper hills. But the usually more level surfaces of the park trails were doable.

She enjoyed matching a trail walk with a visit to a new part of her current county as well as a visit to a new coffee shop or ice cream stand. She had won two cute T-shirts linking the support of local shops with the steps on the trails. She enjoyed eating some sweets from those shops, since she was walking a mile or so to visit them. She also had been able to take some nice photos during the hikes. Maybe she would create a calendar from those nature photos. And another victory of these personal hike challenges was writing her "rhythm poem" for her writer's group. That was a fun result of her nature walks.

Over all, Leise was thankful she still had the stamina and strength to complete this trail challenge. She was proud of the hiking staff with the eleven shields she had earned by completing similar park walks in her previous county. She was determined to earn another staff.

Now, she just had to grin and bear it as she took baby steps on a slow, cold, possibly icy walk to the mailbox. The short trip was certainly not an example of the Sarabande pieces from her Yo-Yo Ma cello CD! She wouldn't hum that fast cello music in her head while walking on such a slippery surface!

Chapter Five

The low tones of the cello were not yet sorrowful, but solemn. Leise had joined over one hundred members of her church in a celebration of a Maundy Thursday service which included a communal dinner and closed with Communion. Remembering the Last Supper was both a thoughtful and joyous occasion for the church members, and the music for the evening after the meal and before the serving of Communion reflected the same emotions.

The cello mourned with the congregation, however, during the Good Friday service. Remembering the crucifixion and burial of their Savior was a serious reflection gathering, and the violin and viola joining their larger brother all played the deeper, lower melodies of the familiar hymns the congregation sang together. Leise reflected again how the instruments helped her worship more deeply during the thoughtful service.

Then came the vibrant, joyous strings of two cellos along with more stringed cousins as well as a French horn and trumpet to loudly celebrate the Risen Lord on Easter Sunday. The auditorium echoed with the singing of the many worshipers and the accompaniments of the instruments' musical support. The cellos also joined in harmony during the adorable children's choir special music presentation.

As Leise walked out of the service, joining in smiling greetings of "Happy Easter!" she saw one of the cellists talking to another orchestra member. The young lady was standing next to her resting instrument now secured in its case. The top of the girl's head was at the same level as the case. The sight made Leise smile even more broadly. It was somehow another symbol for her of the happy celebration of the service that would carry her through the next weeks.

The cello sang as quietly or as loudly as it could for its small human as it shared the music and inspirations of worship with the Lord's body, the Church.

VIOLIN: Rock

Alexxa Burton

His violin sat in the corner gathering a bit more dust every day, its voice silent. Elowin couldn't even bring herself to touch it, to clean it. He had taken ill and died last winter, almost a year ago now, her husband Reynard.

Elowin stood in the dark, looking out the window at more darkness. Winter was approaching again, the edge of cold was in the air with the promise of snow. Those nights of endless snow and dark used to surround them, isolate them into their own little world in these rooms, a world that together they filled with warmth and happiness and music. Elowin used to love those nights, looked forward to winter and the first of its many storms every year when it would blanket the city so deep in snow that nothing moved on the streets and the whole world was only her and Reynard. But that wouldn't come this year. The snow... the snow would still come, and the bracing cold with its fingers that found the gaps in the window frame and worked their way in to caress her skin and make her shiver, but he was no longer there with his music to chase them away and turn the isolation into a thing of joy. In those moments he'd been her whole world. He'd always been her whole world, there'd just been other things that had intruded in on it. Such is the way of life. But her world was gone and it took all her energy simply to face the next breath. She dreaded the coming winter.

Elowin looked back at the dust-covered violin one more time before turning back to the window, her intention to close it, extinguish the candle, and retreat to her bed for another sleepless night. But just before her fingers settled on the latch, she heard something carried to her on the wind. The somber notes of a violin. Her breath caught in her throat and she almost latched the window—unable to listen, the music causing her too much pain. As much as she had longed for it just a moment ago, its sound was like a knife in her heart. Then she recognized the melody. It was one of *his* songs. One that he'd written for her and played for her as they sat on the bank of the river one afternoon shortly after they'd met. It was the song he'd played as she fell in love with him.

She couldn't breathe. It was him. She knew it wasn't, but it was. She had to go to him. It wasn't even a choice.

Her coat was in her hand and she was through the door of her rooms, heading down the wooden stairs that would take her into the city without even realizing she'd moved from the window. She had to find him. It wasn't him, but she had to find him.

She lost her way several times as she wandered the streets of the city; but every time just as she was about to give up and go back, she heard those notes again on the wind. They never changed, it was always the same melody, as if he was playing it over and over, calling to her, and so she made her way through the cold and empty streets, following that call.

The wind was quieting as the dawn approached. She'd been searching all night. Her eyes were heavy and her feet ached but she couldn't face the idea of going back to those empty rooms alone. She sighed, her gaze a cast to the ground in despair and defeat. Slowly, with resignation, she turned. She hadn't heard the music in quite some time. It was time to go back. She couldn't breathe for the pain of it in her chest. Barely able to lift her feet, she began to head back to her rooms. Her rooms, not her home. Her home had disappeared with Reynard.

Before she'd taken a second, shuffling step, something caught her eye. A morning sunbeam on a glint of metal, a pile of trash, discarded and forgotten in the shadowy space between two buildings. But it looked like a hand.

Elowin's breath again caught in her throat and she froze, unable to move. This was what she had been looking for, she knew it, but what was it? Hesitantly, afraid the spell would break, she took one step toward the gap between the buildings. One step, then another. Kneeling down, she reached out to touch the metal hand that had caught her eye, drawing her fingers back quickly as if it were scalding.

Yes, it was definitely metal formed like a hand. The craftsmanship was apparent. All the joints were articulated and proportioned perfectly. But what was the thing?

Carefully, gently, almost lovingly, she extracted the hand from the pile of scrap. An arm followed, severed at the elbow. Pieces of the puzzle began to take shape and make sense before her eyes, a foot, a leg, a knee, bits of another hand, and a head... A head. It was an automaton of some sort.

There was no indication of what its original purpose might have been or how it had ended up in pieces out here on this night. Elowin took off her coat to gather and wrap the pieces so she could carry them all.

Laying her coat out flat on the ground, she realized it had not been her coat she had grabbed off the hook by the door but Reynard's. She nodded. He would need his coat.

With the care that one would give an injured animal, one by one she gathered the pieces of the automaton and laid them on his coat, being careful to the best of her ability to make certain every piece was there and nothing got left behind.

Right hand and arm, she thought, laying the first piece that had caught her eye down carefully. *Two legs and feet, the other hand is broken, where are all the fingers? He must have his fingers, he can't play without his fingers. There, there's the last one. Torso and the other arm, and head of course.*

But what now? She didn't have the skill to fix such a machine. Elowin looked around, uncertain. Did she take the parts home and hope for the best? Would hope, that same force that had pulled her from her rooms and guided her here, be a muse of inspiration and give her the guidance and skill to repair her discovery?

If she couldn't do it, then who? Whose skill could she trust? The clockmaker. If anyone could reassemble this pile of parts, it was the clockmaker. She stood and tenderly held her precious bundle to her chest as she hurried through the streets to the clockmaker's shop. She wanted to be there when he opened.

He was called 'the clockmaker,' but no one could remember the last time he'd made a clock. The window of his shop was filled with all sorts of wonderful things. Assemblies of gears and springs that he'd fashioned into music boxes that put on entire performances with their little characters acting out a ballet as the music played or toys that would mimic an entire circus. If it could be dreamed, the clockmaker could bring it to life with nuts and bolts... and maybe a bit of magic. It was that magic Elowin was counting on now.

She arrived moments after he'd unlocked the shop door. She carried her precious bundle with a pleading look in her eyes.

"Good morning, Elowin. I haven't seen you around town for quite some time. What brings you to my shop so early?" Then, noticing the bundle she carried in her arms, he said, "What do you have there? Let me help with that." The clockmaker came around his workbench to take the automaton parts from her. Elowin was hesitant to surrender them, even if it was her best chance to see him back in working order. "Where did you find all of this?"

"On the street. There's so many pieces. I'm not certain I got them all."

"Anything you missed I either have or can fabricate. It seems you have all the major bits. I wonder who made him and how he got there. This fellow has a story to tell." The clockmaker laid the parts out one by one on his bench.

Elowin's eyes were drawn to a bit of movement in the back corner of the shop. A girl, maybe twelve, was picking through a tray of springs and other bits, her red hair hanging loosely down her back. Noticing her distraction, the clockmaker followed her eyes. "Sarah, leave those alone. I've sorted them already."

The girl only nodded silently before tucking one of the springs into her pocket and disappearing further into the shop.

The clockmaker shook his head. "That girl is as bad as a crow with shiny things."

Elowin's attention turned back to the automaton as the clockmaker laid out the last of the pieces. "Can you fix him?" she asked, desperation in her voice.

"It will be a bit of work, but I should be able to," he answered.

"And he'll be able to do everything as before?" Elowin reached out to touch the broken left hand. "The violin, he must be able to play his violin."

The clockmaker gave Elowin a long look. "This won't bring him back, this isn't Reynard. It would be like settling for a rock. You can't do that."

Elowin's eyes snapped up, giving the clockmaker a look that could turn hell to ice. "Then rock it is," she snapped. "But you can fix him?"

Resigned, he nodded. "The repairs should be done in a week."

She let out a sigh of relief. "He will be recovered in a week. Thank you."

As Elowin turned to leave, he called out after her, "Your coat, it's cold outside."

She shook her head and continued out the door. "He will need his coat."

For the first time in a year, she felt like she could breathe, felt the warmth of the sun on her skin, felt the weight on her shoulder that had been crushing her a bit more each day lifted. She smiled at the people on the street and they smiled back. The birds sang their songs and going up the steps to her room didn't feel like descending into the madness of hell, it felt like coming up for air.

Once again standing in her room, she turned and looked at his violin sitting in the corner, covered in dust. "Well that just won't do," she said aloud. He would be so angry if he came home and found his beautiful instrument in such a state.

Elowin picked up the violin lovingly and carefully, and ever so methodically cleaned it, removing every speck of dust and polishing the wood till it shone again. Taking up the bow, with skill he had taught her, she adjusted the tension on its horsehair strings and continued to tune the violin until the notes it produced were pure and clear as glass. Perfect. He would be happy.

Then she looked slowly around the room. When had it gotten so bad? She couldn't let him come home to this. A plume of dust billowed from the curtains as she pulled them back, letting the sun stream into the shadows and letting her have a proper look at the condition of things. Everything was covered in the same layer of dust as the violin. There were cobwebs, some also caked with dust, hanging from every corner. The candles on the table were down to dregs, the sink was full of plates and glasses and remnants of food, the sheets on the bed were stained with wine and tears.

Elowin nodded, resolute that these rooms would shine like his violin by the time he came home. So much to do. Not just the cleaning, but washing as well. Surely his clothing in the wardrobe smelled of dust and mothballs, and there wasn't a crumb of food in the house. How could she possibly make them a proper dinner that way? And wine, they would need wine to celebrate his homecoming.

Despite the growing chill in the air, the next week felt like Elowin was stepping out into a bright spring morning. There were happy people everywhere and Elowin was one of them. The sun was bright, the food had flavor, the world had music again. Her small, dark rooms had been scrubbed top to bottom and the curtains thrown back to flood the place with sunlight. Every scrap of clothing and linens had been washed and ironed, she had even gotten a bundle of dried lavender to hang in the wardrobe, its sweet smell permeating the apartment. There was food in her cupboards and a lovely bottle of wine waiting on the table and she was on her way to the butcher to purchase a whole chicken to roast for dinner. His homecoming would be a joyful occasion indeed.

The rest of the day was filled with preparations. Elowin was so excited she could barely hold her knife steady as she chopped the vegetables for the chicken. There was fresh baked bread and an apple pie, his favorite. She must have rewashed the wine goblets half a dozen times before she was satisfied with the way they shone in the light. She cleaned and tuned his violin again as she had every day since finding him, and changed the sheets on the bed no less than three times before she was convinced she'd chosen the right ones. She put on her best dress, the one with the maroon skirt she wore at Christmas, and tied her hair back at the base of her neck the way he'd always liked it.

Elowin arrived at the clockmaker's shop an hour before he closed. She had wanted to give him as much time as possible to work his particular magic. The automaton was sitting, complete and whole in a chair at the back of the shop, staring off blankly into the shadows. She rushed over to him immediately, dropping to her knees and taking his hands in hers, trying to hold back her tears.

"He's perfect, absolutely perfect. You are an angel and a miracle worker, Mr. Clockmaker." She lovingly helped the automaton into Reynard's coat before the clockmaker offered her a bulky leather bag.

"These are his music, so he can play."

"Thank you so much sir, we can never repay you, no amount of money could possibly be enough," said Elowin, pressing the money she'd brought into his hands.

"Elowin, you know he's not—"

She cut off the clockmaker, "He is healthy and whole and we will have the rest of our lives together thanks to you."

The leather bag swung over her shoulder, she tucked her arm into the automaton's and guided him out the door and down the street to their home.

They walked slowly, Elowin taking the time to point out all their favorite places, the bakery that had his favorite pastries, the river where they'd so often sat as he played for her, the square where the Christmas market was held every year. The streets were dark by the time they finally climbed the steps to their rooms.

It was far past a normal time for dinner, but Elowin prepared two plates. Sitting across from him at the table she didn't even notice that he didn't touch the food in front of him. They sat in silence, Elowin unable to tear her eyes from his face, reveling in the simple fact of his presence. They sat there till the brand-new candles burned themselves out and the wine was long gone.

"It's gotten so late! Where has the time gone? Don't worry about a thing, just sit there and I'll clean all of this up, then we can go to bed."

She put away the last of the chicken and pie and wrapped the bread to make toast in the morning. All the while he sat there silent and still, staring straight ahead at nothing as he had been the entire evening. She knelt to build a fire in the hearth and soon the dancing flames chased the chill from the air.

"I know it's late and you must be tired, but it's been so very long. Will you play me just one song to fall asleep to?"

He didn't answer her, but stood as she bid him and followed her to the bed. Elowin sat him on the edge of the bed and lifted his violin for him to see.

"I cleaned and tuned it just as you taught me. It's all ready for you." She carefully put the violin into place, his hand on the neck and the chin rest set firmly against his lower jaw. Taking one of the metal cylinders from the leather bag the clockmaker had given her, she inserted it into the automaton's back, then turned the clockwork that would allow him to play.

His fingers moved on the strings and he moved the bow back and forth producing notes, pure and beautiful. The sound filled the room and overflowed Elowin's heart.

She, oh so gently, kissed him on the cheek before lying down in the bed. "Good night, Rock. I love you." Then she reached her arm out so her fingertips just brushed his leg, not enough to distract him but enough to reassure her that he was still there and hadn't disappeared into the night.

Her breathing grew deep and steady as she fell asleep, the first truly deep and restful sleep she'd had in a year. And he continued to play, the notes swirling around the room and finding the gaps in the window frame and tumbling out into the street below as if they had a life of their own.

As he played, his head slowly turned, and he looked down at the sleeping Elowin.

SAXOPHONE: Root Beer Dreams

Donna J. Bunner

"Oh no. Not today. Please car keep going. Of all days..." Maddie reluctantly pulled the car over as all the dashboard lights flashed red and yellow. She pressed her head against the steering wheel and cried out, "What am I going to do? I can't miss this meeting. I don't know how I'll pay to get this fixed. I only have five dollars to my checking account. Oh geez. I can't afford to miss work. Maybe I can take a vacation day. Oh, brother."

Just then, there was a knock on Maddie's window. Maddie startled. An older gentleman appeared at the window with a look of concern on his face. "Ma'am, are you alright?"

Maddie hit the button to roll down her window. "Yes, yes. No. I don't know. I was just driving along when all a sudden the dashboard lights came on and the car came to a halt and just stopped. I normally don't drive this way to work, but I woke up late this morning, and I thought this would be a shortcut to get out of the expressway traffic."

"Well, out here in the country we don't see too many cars, but we've been seeing more lately since they've been working on the expressway. I walked into the garage and noticed your car along side the road. May I be of some help? By the way, my name is Gus."

"Thanks, thanks so much. My name is Maddie, Maddie Chambers. I work at Kellogg's Bank & Trust down the road here. Figures, I have an important meeting today, and my car had to act up."

"I could have my son look at it. He is on his way over to try to fix my lawn mower that's been acting up. I could take you to work or he could, if you don't mind," Gus said.

"That would be wonderful. I only have five dollars until payday. I could pay you then," Maddie said.

"Don't worry about it until we see what's going on. Oh good, here comes Greg now."

A blue Range Rover suddenly pulled up in the driveway. Maddie recognized Greg immediately as he was a frequent customer at the bank. Maddie's co-workers would *ohh* and *aah* over him, and according, to them, Greg had the fanciest car around town. Not to mention his piercing, blue eyes. He always had a tortoiseshell cat lying beside him in the car.

"Why, hello there stranger. Are you off from the bank today?" Greg asked, getting out of the car.

"Hello there Mr. Struthers. No. Not today. I was on my way to work when my car suddenly died on me. Gus came out and tried to help," Maddie explained.

"I told Maddie that you may be able to look at it, if that's okay. I was going to take her to work while you look at that and my old lawn mower," Gus said.

"Well, I can take her to work Dad. That is, if you don't mind?" Greg asked.

All the sudden, Maddie felt something rubbing around her legs, going round and round. Maddie looked down and noticed it was a tortoiseshell cat. "Why, aren't you a pretty girl? I always see you when you come through the bank. Your name is Whiskers, isn't it?"

"Whiskers, what are you doing out of the car? Oh my goodness." Greg picked up the cat and put her in the back seat of the Ranger Rover. "Sorry girl, you'll have to ride in the back seat so this pretty lady here can sit in the front."

"Thanks again so much for the ride, Mr. Struthers. I really appreciate it."

"Think nothing of it. I usually have Tuesdays off and spend time with my Dad. Since my Mom died six months ago, I really worry about him being alone."

"I'm sorry to hear about your Mom passing. Please accept my condolences, Mr. Struthers."

"Please, Maddie, call me Greg."

"Alright then... Greg." She paused. "Speaking of Whiskers, she must be your buddy since she is always with you when you come through our bank drive-through."

"Yes. Whiskers suddenly showed up at my doorstep and has been with me ever since. She goes with me everywhere."

With a smile Maddie said, "I'm glad you have Whiskers as your furry companion and friend."

Greg started backing out of the driveway when Maddie heard the most beautiful sound that she ever heard. It sounded like a horn of some kind. Maddie turned around in her seat and noticed Whiskers playing a brass instrument. "Is is that a saxophone Whiskers is playing?"

"Yes. Please don't be alarmed. I previously played in the orchestra but ceased performing approximately two years ago. When Whiskers arrived at my home, she consistently chose to rest atop my saxophone case. Eventually, I decided to play the instrument for her, until one day, while answering a phone call in the kitchen, I left my saxophone in its case. During the call, I unexpectedly heard saxophone music coming from the living room. Upon returning, I observed Whiskers actively playing the instrument. Although initially quite astonishing, I have since become accustomed to this behavior."

"How can a cat play an instrument? I didn't think that was possible. Are you still in the orchestra?" Maddie asked.

"No, I retired from that position three years ago when my wife became ill," Greg explained. "After her passing, I assumed responsibility for Dad's construction business so that he could transition into semi-retirement. Although I have encouraged him to reduce his workload, he continues to work as much as I do." Whiskers kept softly playing the yellow saxophone. Maddy was enjoying the music so much that Greg had to tap Maddie's shoulder and said, "We're here at the bank Maddie I will let you know about your car as soon as I look over it and see if I can figure out what's wrong with it."

"Oh sorry," Maddie said as she fumbled for her keys in her work purse. "Thanks so much. I could listen to Whiskers play all day. I still can't believe it. Thanks for the ride." Maddie jumped out of Greg's car and ran to get to the time clock so she wouldn't be late. "Geez. Thank the Lord. Only one minute to spare," Maddie said to herself.

Maddie walked into her office, she sat at her desk, and sighed. *Only me, only me.* She grabbed her clipboard and headed to the front to see where the tellers were.

"Who was that hottie that dropped you off?" Rhonda asked.

"Was that Mr. Struthers?" Samantha asked.

"Guys, please. Yes. It was Mr. Struthers's car. My car broke down this morning in front of his dad's house, and Mr. Struthers just happened to show up in the driveway."

"Sounds like a start to a fairytale to me," Rhonda said wistfully.

Just then, Mr. Walker, their boss, opened his door. "Ladies, I'm cancelling this morning's meeting. I have an emergency at home."

"Oh my. I hope everything is alright, Mr. Walker," Maddie said.

"Well, Minnie, our snickerdoodle, got hit by a car."

Gasping and *awwww*s were heard among the tellers.

"Melody is with her now at the vet hospital. It looks as if it is just a broken leg. Since that is Melody's baby, I'd better head over there to make sure everything is alright with both of my beauties."

"That's so sweet Mr. Walker," Makayla said coming out of her office.

"Thank ya kindly. Before I go, Maddie can I see you in my office?"

"Sure thing Mr. Walker." As Maddie started walking toward Mr. Walkers office, she turned her head toward Makayla and raised her eyebrows.

"Well, now Maddie have a seat," Mr. Walker said while gesturing his hand toward the chair. "Maddie, you're probably wondering why I called you in my office. I know you just moved here not too long ago, but you've been doing a fine job, a fine job. I was thinking about offering you an assistant loan officer position. You would be assisting Makayla. It seems our branch is growing, and we need someone who could help assist processing loans."

Maddie was shocked. "Why yes, I would be interested. Loans were my expertise at my former banking position before I moved."

"I know. With your experience and expertise, I think that this position will suit you just fine. Of course, we'll talk about the position more in detail when I get back in the office on Monday. Money should be more, of course."

"Thank you for thinking of me, Mr. Walker. I look forward to it. I hope your wife and puppy will be okay."

"Thank you Maddie. Have a nice weekend."

Maddie shook hands with Mr. Walker and left his office. It was almost time for lunch. Maddie decided to walk to her office before she had to cover Della and Makayla for lunch breaks.

As Maddie entered her office, she noticed a red light flashing on her phone, signaling there was a voice message. As Maddie pressed the button to listen to her message there were no words; only the sound of saxophone music. Maddie saved the message as the music had been so beautiful. Then Maddie heard a male's voice starting the next message, "Hey, this is Greg. Your car is fixed and is in the parking lot at your bank. I put the keys under the driver's mat. It was your alternator. Usually when the alternator is bad your battery would be the next to go, so I replaced them both. Don't worry about paying me. Just come down and hear me play some time at Dunkin Valley Café tonight. I usually play there every Friday night. Hopefully I'll see you tonight or soon at the café. God bless."

Boy, it didn't take him long to fix my car. Woohoo. One less thing to worry about.

As Maddie hung up the receiver, she wasn't sure what to do. *I owe Greg something for fixing my car. I can't expect him to fix it for free. I need to go to the café tonight. There's something about this car. There's something about Greg too. I should thank him in person, right? I haven't been on a date in two years. Wait. Is this a date?* She checked the time. *Well, off to the lobby.*

Well I better get ready. It's 5:30. I'll go to the restaurant a little early to get a seat and scope out the place. Am I doing the right thing? Maddie pulled out a pair of jeans and a red cardigan to wear.

Maddie got into her car and started to pull out of her driveway when a blue Range Rover pulled in behind her. It was Greg. Greg got out of his car and approached the driver's side of hers. Maddie hit the button to roll down her window. "Why hello there," Maddie said.

"I hope I didn't startle you. I found your driver's license in my car. It must've fell out of your purse when you were getting out of my car this morning," Greg said handing her the driver's license.

"Oh geez. I didn't even realize it was gone. Thank you so much. First for fixing my car and now bringing me my license. Words cannot say how much I appreciate you," Maddie said.

"Think nothing of it. Say, I hope you were coming down to the café tonight."

"Why yes, that is where I was heading. I didn't just want to thank you personally for fixing my car, I also wanted to try this root beer that everyone has been talking about."

Greg laughed and said, "It's been in my family for generations. It's been my great grandmother's special recipe." Greg looked down at his watch and said, "Time's a-wasting. I must run. Hey, do you want to ride with me down to the café? I decided not to play tonight. I only plan on stopping in and checking on things. I have a purchase order that needs signed, and a few other things to take care of."

"I would hate to be a bother at your work and all," Maggie said.

"No bother at all. Besides, I think Whiskers wants you to come along." Whiskers was standing beside Greg, licking her paws.

"Well, if its okay with Whiskers, it's okay with me," Maggie said.

Maddie pulled her car up and closed the garage door behind her. As soon as Maddie got into the passenger side of the car, Whiskers jumped on Maddie's lap.

"Well, I think you have a new friend," Greg said.

As they drove, they talked about their previous lives: how Greg's wife had died from lung cancer a year prior and how Maddie broke up from a relationship from her high school sweetheart six months earlier and moving away to get a fresh start when she got her new job at the bank.

An hour had passed before Greg pulled into the Dunkin Valley Café. As they walked into the café, the restaurant had a few customers but not as busy as Maddie would think for a Friday night. Greg walked Maddie over to a table close to the kitchen. "Go ahead and have a seat. I'll check on a few things and be right back with you."

As Greg walked away, Maddie pulled her phone out of her purse to play solitaire while she waited for Greg to come back. Half an hour went by, and Maddie decided to go to the restroom to freshen up. As Maddie stood up, she bumped into Greg, who was carrying two mugs in his hands. "Whoa whoa," Greg said as he turned around saving the drinks from falling out of his hands.

"I am so sorry, Greg. I am so sorry." Maddie's face reddened from embarrassment.

"No worries. We made the save." Greg winked at her. "If you're looking for the restroom, they are right over there."

When Maddie returned from the restroom, she started to walk over to the table. She noticed from a distance a vase of roses along with two mugs of root beer. There was also a dinner plate with a cheeseburger and fries. Greg was sitting at the table with Whiskers on his lap. “I hope you like cheeseburgers. I had the cook make some for us,” Greg said.

“I love cheeseburgers. Thank you very much. The roses are beautiful.”

“You are more than welcome. You had better like the root beer the most.” Greg chuckled.

Maddie raised her mug to make a toast when she heard saxophone music again. She looked all around and didn’t see who was playing. “Yummy. This is so good. Now I know nobody is lying when they say this is the best root beer.”

“I’m glad you like,” Greg said.

“Hey, Greg. Where is that music coming from? Is that Whiskers?” Maddie asked.

Greg pointed to the stage and noticed that Whiskers was playing along with a soul song. Maddie didn’t even notice that Whiskers had gotten off of Greg’s lap.

“Can you tell me how a cat can play a saxophone? I am dying to know,” Maddie asked.

Beep. Beep. It sounded like an alarm clock. *It can't be. What time is it?* Maddie thought groggily. *Where am I?* Maddie looked around. She was in her bedroom. She rose up from her bed and turned off the alarm. It was 2:30 in the morning. *Did I really dream of all of that? My car dying, a promotion, a date, and a cat playing saxophone?*

Maddie jumped out of bed. She wanted to make sure her car would start. *Did my car really break down? Was this all really a dream?*

Maddie grabbed her keys from the kitchen counter. She noticed a mug of root beer sitting beside her keys. Beside the mug, there was a note that read, *Never give up hope.*

Okay. This is strange. Did I really ride with Greg to the restaurant? Did I really see a cat playing a saxophone?

As Maddie walked out to the garage, she opened her car door and noticed another mug of root beer in her front cup holder console. There laid a rose beside it with another note that read, *Life has many questions and challenges. Walk each day like a dream with your head held high.*

Okay. What's going on? I couldn't be making all of this stuff up. Maddie turned the key, and the car started right up. The radio turned on and instrumental saxophone music was playing. All Maddie could do is laugh. "Okay. Back to bed I go."

Maddie got out of her car and went back into the house. *Boy when I dream I really dream. I guess I'll have to keep dreaming big. I hope I got the promotion. Oh man.* Maddie went back into the house and found her purse. She remembered that Mr. Walker had given her a new job description and other paperwork to sign in a blue folder. Maddie opened her purse and found the folder. "Well, at least that part of the dream is true."

Morale of the story, when you only have $5 to your name, cars can still get repaired, promotions can still happen, and dates can take place. Continue to dream big dreams, hold onto your faith, hold your head up high, and don't forget to drink root beer and jam to classical saxophone music.

GUITAR: Interlude of Joy

Barbara Lang

From an outsider's perspective, dairy farming may look like it belongs in a Hallmark Christmas movie. Cows grazing in a verdant pasture in front of picturesque red barn with a tree-lined driveway winding its way to a pretty white farmhouse is an illusion.

Sadly, the days of the small family dairy are giving way to large operations of 1,000 or more cows in order to be profitable. And with good employees nearly impossible to find, the majority of milkers are immigrants.

Although our herd hovered around 200, we needed dependable milkers. I didn't want to give up my job to be a full-time farm worker. We had exhausted the local labor force and had one bad experience after another with employees who stole, lied, left without notice, wrecked machinery and buildings, and a meth head who tried to kill my husband. We finally gave up and hired our first immigrant. He was a lifesaver and a refreshing change from our previous shady workforce. But all good things must come to an end, and our first hardworking immigrant left us for a better job in a factory.

After several frustrating fifteen-hour work days and calling and emailing all my contacts, through a middleman, I found two Mexican immigrants who could start that weekend. The morning they showed up in a 2004 Hummer made me slightly nervous, but I was so happy to see them, I didn't care. It wasn't long before the quieter one became my favorite. Instead of dreading chores, I began to look forward to working with him. He was energetic, happy, quick, and efficient at his job. It was a joy to hear him singing as he worked and for the first time, I had fun in the barns. He was an excellent cook and sometimes shared his meal with me and helped to plant flowers around the buildings. All the other workers we had hired only wanted to do the bare minimum, not caring about anything but their paychecks.

He wanted to become a US citizen, and in the spring I began taking him to English classes along with another young man after the owner of the Hummer left to go back to his previous job and gringa girlfriend in upstate New York.

During the forty minute car trips back and forth to the lessons, he shared details with me of his family and about growing up in Mexico. It was horrific to hear about the risks he had endured to come to America. He could only bring the bare minimum when he crossed the desert and almost died. He wished he had his guitar, but he had to leave it behind. When he was young, he was a musician in a group and had even written a hit song when he was a teenager, but it was stolen by another band. I surprised him with my old guitar on his birthday. He thanked me profusely and promised me he would play the song he wrote on his next day off.

But I never got to hear him play. The next week the day after payday, the milking parlor was dark when I drove to the farm to feed calves. When he didn't show up after I had milked the first group of cows, I went to the house to wake him up. I called his name from the kitchen several times, but no one answered. When I went to look in his room, my heart sank when I realized both workers had left. Everything they owned and the guitar were gone too.

I never got attached to employees and he even told me when he first started that he was just passing through but I didn't take his words to heart. I had fooled myself into thinking he would never leave me without a goodbye and this was the deepest cut.

I always held out hope he would come back, but I never heard from him again. Sometimes I think I see him in the shadows when I'm in the calf barn or the milking parlor. But it's only my imagination and wishful thinking. New employees have come and gone, but I know that I'll never find anyone like him ever again.

When I see something on Facebook about another ICE raid, it makes my blood boil that these goons are targeting good people because of the color of their skin.

I worry about him and hope that he is safely back in Mexico playing his guitar and singing with his band again. He made me a better person and gave me the little he had that was worth all the gold in the world, an interlude of joy.

FLUTE: Ollie and Artie

Donna J. Bunner

OUR STORY BEGINS WITH a hippopotamus named Ollie, whose favorite spot to lay is a purple raft in the muddy swamp behind the Wilson family house. Ollie loved living in this particular swamp, as each day brought a new adventure of stories to tell with all of his friends who lived around the swamp. On most days, Ollie swam around the swamp by himself, enjoying the peace and quiet the swamp life brought.

On this particular morning, a moving van showed up. Ollie immediately sunk beneath the lakeweed and branches until only his eyes showed above the swampy water. Ollie watched as people kept coming in and out of the tiny blue house that sat vacant for what seemed like years. After

Grandma Wilson died, he wondered what would happen to his beloved swamp and if he would have to move again someday. Ollie reminisced about the huge chocolate chip cookies that Grandma Wilson used to bring him. He also missed the late-night music of violin strings as he would mull around in the swamp taking his late night bath. Ollie continued to watch all the boxes and furniture coming into the house when all of a sudden Ollie heard a horn of some sort sound off in the distance. The sound was just beautiful.

Ollie started to move closer to the dry land when he heard a voice, "Hey, hey you. What's your name?"

Ollie looked around and didn't see anyone.

He heard the voice again. "Over here. Yoo-hoo!" Ollie finally glanced over to a nearby tree and saw a gray and black tabby cat sitting on a branch with a silver object in its paws. That beautiful sound could be heard again and again as the cat put the silver object to its lips and blew, making the most beautiful melody in the atmosphere.

"Oh, hi. There you are. I'm Ollie. I've never seen you around here before."

"Yeah. I'm Artie. I just moved here with my family over there."

"I've seen the people and boxes over there," Ollie replied.

"If you see a calico cat roaming around here, too, that's my sister Sparkles. She's been upset since the move. We'd lived at our old house since we were born, so she's taking this move hard. I always play my flute when she gets upset. That's the only thing that calms her down".

"I was wondering what that silver thing was. The sound that comes out that thing is so beautiful," Ollie said.

"Thank you. Thank you very much. I used to hear our owner playing it and kept watching until I learned to play it myself."

"Does your owner know you play?" Ollie asked.

"Yes. I just picked up the flute in the middle of the night and started playing it. I woke her up from a deep sleep, and she watched me in amazement. Our owner used to play in symphonic orchestras all over the world. Her last time playing was in New York a couple of months ago, until tragedy struck—the reason we moved here all the way to the boondocks."

"What happened, Artie?" Ollie asked. "That is, if you want to talk about it."

"Well, Marcia, our owner was in a car accident, and her fiancé was killed. Marcia was in the hospital for two weeks getting her strength back. She hasn't picked up any of her instruments since. It's like she gave up on life. We moved here to Louisiana to her grandparents' vacation house to get away from the hustle and bustle of New York for a fresh start."

"Marcia must be Grandma Wilson's granddaughter. I heard her speak of Marcia often. I've only been here at the swamp a couple of years myself. I was dropped off in this swamp. I would always hear Grandma Wilson playing a violin off into the night."

"Yes, music must be a family trait for sure," Artie said. "Hey, let me ask you something: What is it like down here, you know, living by the swamp?"

"Well, it's pretty quiet for sure, so Marcia should have plenty of quiet time to get settled," Ollie answered. "I have to tell you that I am good at storytelling."

"Story telling?" Artie asked.

"Why yes, I retell all the stories that Grandma Wilson used to tell throughout this swampland. I usually get Rodney the Raccoon, Jake the Snake, Florence and Ben, from the beaver family that live down the swap aways. Usually, once a night, we all gather and story-time begins."

"Did I hear stories? I love stories," a cat said as she pounced on Artie and knocked him to the ground. "Gotcha bro. I gotcha!" Artie swatted back at the cat and chased after her.

"Well, I guess this is Sparkles?" Ollie asked.

"You betcha," Sparkles answered, still running and pouncing.

Artie stopped running and said, "Sparkles, this is Ollie. Ollie, this is Sparkles."

"Nice to meet you, furball," Ollie said

"Furball? Who are you calling furball?"

Ollie let out a belly laugh and answered, "You, of course. I can tell you're the ornery one in the family."

"What's the story for today, Ollie? I'm like Sparkles. I *love* stories." Artie said.

"Well, I can tell you the story I told the gang last night, but I can't finish it until tonight."

"Oh, why not? Come on now, Ollie," Sparkles said excitedly.

"Well, I don't like to repeat myself for one. And another, the rest of the gang look forward to my stories and probably want to hear the rest of it, too. Like I said, I'm the best storyteller in the swampland."

"Well, let's hear it," Artie said. "I may add some music if I see fit."

"Very well. Sit down in the grass, relax, and open your ears to the greatest storyteller ever.

"Our story begins with a girl named Marcia."

"Hey, our owner is Marcia," Artie said and then blew a note from his flute.

"Yes, that's right," Ollie said. "Marcia was inside her house doing dishes when she heard the doorbell ring. She went to the door and opened it. No one was there. She closed the door and started to walk back to the kitchen when the doorbell rang again. Marcia went to the front door once again and opened it. No one was there. Marcia stepped outside and looked around to see if she could see or find anything outside. When she turned around to go back inside, she looked down at her feet and noticed a white rose lying on the doormat.

"*That is very strange,* Marcia thought.

"'Hello? Hello? Anyone there?' Marcia stooped down to pick up the rose when she heard the stomping of feet approaching. Then she heard neighing. As Marcia straightened, there stood the most beautiful white horse."

"You gotta watch them creatures. They can pounce on you in a second," Artie said.

"Anyway, the horse's mane was as white as snow," Ollie continued on with his story. "'Why hello there. Are you lost pretty one?' Marcia asked.

"All of a sudden, a pink nose was nudging Marcia's hand. As Marcia started to scratch the horse's ear, the horse moved its head from her reach and bent down, picking up the white rose and beginning to run away. The horse moved a few feet, stopped, and turned back to look at

Marcia. Then it started walking again, to only stop, look again, and repeat.

"I think this horse wants me to follow it, Marcia thought.

"Artie came to the door to scope out the situation. Marcia and Artie decided to follow the horse."

"Hey, that's my name! I bet I'm better looking," Artie said.

"In your dreams." Sparkles laughed. "Go on with your story, Ollie."

"Marcia decided to follow the horse. 'Well buddy. Show me the way.'

"With the white rose in the horse's mouth, the horse led the way down the gravel road. All of a sudden, Sparkles pounced on Artie, knocking her to the ground.

"'You guys thought you were going without me, didn't ya?' Sparkles said to Artie.

"'You're a silly goose,' Artie replied."

"Hey, I'm in the story, too. Ollie? Are you making this up as you go? I don't think there would ever be another Artie and Sparkles like us," Sparkles said.

"I said I was the best storyteller in the swampland, didn't I? May I continue or should I wait until tonight?" Ollie asked.

"No, no please go on," Artie answered. "Sparkles, quit interrupting".

"Hey, I had an important question to ask. I thought I had better ask before I forget it," Sparkles said.

"Well, as I will continue. Oh brother. Well the horse suddenly stopped its walk and started to turn to the left, down a gravel driveway. Marcia looked over at a nearby maple tree and noticed a violin lying on the tree branches."

"'What is this? A violin lying out in the middle of nowhere?'

"Marcia picked up the violin and began to look it over. As Marcia turned the violin, she noticed a card taped to the back of the violin.

"'What in the world?'

"She removed the card and began to open it. There was an inscription on the back of the envelope that read *My dearest Marcia.*

"'My name on the envelope? What's going on?'

"Marcia's hands began to tremble as she opened the envelope. As Marcia took the card out, she noticed a white rose that has been dried and glued to the top. Marcia opened the card and started to read the black ink writing.

"*My dearest Marcia, I hope this card finds you well years after it was written. I decided to leave your Grandmother. Not because I didn't love her, but because she wouldn't pursue her love for the orchestra and play her Daddy's violin if I stayed. I didn't want her to miss playing in the harmonic orchestra. I missed watching you grow up. Please forgive me, as I did what I thought was best. I love you with all my heart. Take this key and unlock the trunk inside the old farm house. Know that I loved you very much. Love you always, Tim Gallagher.*

"Marcia removed the key from the card, closed it, and wiped the tears from her eyes.

"The card was for her mother Marcia. Marcia remembered her mom speak of her great grandfather leaving her great grandmother when she was six years old. She never understood the reasoning until now. Tim Gallagher was her great grandfather's pen name he used during his days in the orchestra. Great grandmother was always jealous of Tim's success. And when he received a job offer to teach in Boston, he left in the middle of the night. He knew that if he stayed, great grandmother would never practice and pursue her dream. She was competitive in that way.

"Marcia stood up from beneath the maple tree. With the violin in one hand and the key in the other, Marcia once again followed the horse up the long narrow driveway. In the distance, Marcia could see an old, abandoned farmhouse that was a dirty-white color with two of the shutters half-hanging from the front of the house. Marcia approached the steps that led to the front porch. She hesitated for a minute when she felt a nose touching her backside, nudging her.

"Marcia started to laugh. 'Alright already. Give me a minute.'

"The horse neighed and nudged her again. Marcia walked into the porch and approached the half-opened front door before opening it and walking in. As it squeaked open, Marcia wondered what she was doing and what the key in her hand opened. She walked through the living room and noticed an old oak chest sitting on a dark-colored coffee table.

"'I wonder if this is what the key unlocks?'

"Marcia inserted the key into the keyhole that was on the front of the chest. The lid opened. She lifted the lid and couldn't believe her eyes. Piles of $100 bills. Marcia exclaimed in excitement."

"What's she going to do with all of that money, Ollie? Do you think she will share? What do you think, Ollie, huh huh?"

"Let me continue, Artie. Let me continue," Ollie said.

"Marcia immediately closed the lid. Artie and Sparkles jumped up on the coffee table sniffing the trunk as if to investigate. Marcia walked around the corner into the kitchen and noticed the kitchen table that had plates and silverware set perfectly, like a special dinner was about to be served."

"I wonder if someone was there and left for a while. Huh? What do you think Ollie?" Artie asked.

"Oh dear. I'm never going to finish my story at this rate," Ollie said, shaking his head.

"Marcia left the kitchen and walked back toward the treasure chest and stood for a moment, not knowing what to do. *Should I take the money or just walk out of here and pretend nothing happened?*

"Marcia decided to lock the chest and walk out of the house. When Marcia walked out the door and down the steps, the white horse could not be found. *Where could that horse have gone?*

"Marcia walked down the steps, stood for a moment, and looked around. The horse was nowhere to be found. Marcia decided to head home and pretend like nothing happened. As Marcia passed the tree, she realized that she placed the violin on the coffee table next to the trunk. *Oh well, time for home.*

"Marcia, Artie, and Sprinkles walked down the gravel road to their house. Marcia went to unlock the door when she noticed a violin lying there with the note and the white rose.

"'What in the world? Is that the violin I left inside the old farmhouse?' Marcia asked. 'Come on Artie and Sprinkles. I bet you two are starving. It's treat time.'"

"I love that our names are being used in the story, Sparkles," Artie said.

"Me too," Sparkles said.

Suddenly, Ollie stood up from the grassy hill he was lying on and said, "Well, enough of this daytime story-telling. If you want to know what happened next, you'll have to come back down to the swamp to hear the rest."

Ollie started walking on the edge of his home of swampy water when all of a sudden he heard Artie playing his flute. Sparkles started meowing and jumping up and down on all four paws and then said, "Please continue Ollie. I like the story so far. I can't wait until tonight."

"Patience is a virtue, my dear new friend. Tonight it is." Ollie slid down in the swamp until all that was seen was his two eyes sticking out of the water.

"What do you think of all of this, Artie? Our names in this story, and we didn't even hear the ending. Is this a true story?" Sparkles said.

"Well, Sparkles, I think it's a mystery. A white rose and a white horse and a treasure of money. I think they are symbols of some sort. I guess we won't know what they mean until tonight. I guess I'll keep playing my melody and wait until tonight."

All of a sudden, a white horse started walking toward Artie and Sparkles.

"Look, Artie! There's a white horse. This must be a true story," Sparkles said

"Not until tonight," the white horse said. "Not until tonight."

HARP: Oblivion!!

Bill Reid

A SHADOWY FIGURE IS EMERGING FROM yet another red dust and debris storm. The storm was caused by a large, red object that came from above. He is still confused and disoriented, before the last storm he was on a yellow surface. Now, looking down, he sees a white surface, but with the same equally-spaced blue lines going off into the distance.

The man's name is "Adrian French," but he hasn't realized it yet. As he is trying to gain his bearings, Adrian is engulfed in the same grayish mist and grayish, dim light above, as numerous times before.

Suddenly, out of nowhere, a long, yellow pole (along with a loud babble from above) with a black point hits the white surface next to Adrian.

The yellow pole moves along between the blue lines. The man is beginning to comprehend his surroundings. Thoughts and words are formed in his head, but from an outside source. As the yellow pole moves along the white surface, the gray mist is lifting and becoming much brighter. The words are clearer now. In his mind, he realized who he is; "Adrian French." Now his story can begin again, in his own words.

Figuratively Speaking

My name is "Adrian French," ex-CIA agent (without portfolio) and fugitive wanted by the same agency. The trouble began three or four weeks ago. I was assigned to apprehend a renegade ex-KGB agent. Being a "hot shot" agent (in my own mind) I did not request backup, as required by protocol. When I arrived at the location in Upper Manhattan, my quarry was long gone.

After an internal investigation of this fiasco, I was relieved of duty and put on ice. The results of the inquiry revealed a certain female companion of mine (who turned out to be a double agent) facilitated his escape into the unknown. She was no angel, but she played me like a harp.

Fortunately, I was confined to my apartment, as the agency wanted to avoid any publicity concerning the endeavor. Although I was being watched intensely, I needed a plan to escape and redeem myself.

The heart of my escape plan involved the history of my ground-floor apartment. During the 1920s Prohibition, the apartment became a "speakeasy[1]." A group of nightclub owners, some questionable city officials, and other "interested parties" purchased a few brownstones throughout the city.

The group wanted to turn the ground-floor apartments into small "nightspots" or "after-hours clubs."

When Prohibition raised its ugly head, remodeling now included hidden passageways between the buildings.[2]

With the repeal of Prohibition, the "speakeasies" were remodeled back to their previous lives. My apartment turned out to be an exception by chance of oversight. The hidden passage was never touched. It was by pure luck that I found some old blueprints showing the exact loca-

---

1. During the height of the Prohibition, there were 32,000 speakeasies in the city of New York.

2. Not all buildings were changed, just a few in prominent locations. Rumrunners and speakeasy operators could move booze, beer, etc. between the buildings without being detected (the passageways were also used to move a few well known "celebrities" during so called "police raids.")

tion of the passageway. I told nobody of this hidden gem (including my female companions).

Every day and night my "watch dogs" would check the elaborate locking system on all windows and outside doors (to make sure I did not tamper with them).

The night I put my escape plan into motion was no exception. The only variable, a gale-like storm hovering over the city.

Darkness was falling when my watch dogs finally left to hunker down in other parts of the building. But they'd be back around 9:00am the next day.

It was time to move and move fast. In the passageway, I retrieved an overnight bag I had stashed a couple weeks before. The bag contained some nondescript clothes, passports and IDs, and a small makeup kit. The kit contained odds and ends to slightly change my appearance. This item came about after reading the memoirs of an O.S.S. agent.

Locking the mechanism from the inside to conceal the entrance, I hurried through the passageway. The exit came out into a blind alley between two buildings down the block. Locking and concealing the doorway, I hustled to the mouth of the alley and into a blinding rainstorm. No sane person would, or should, have been out on a night like that.

Rain pummeled me from all angles as I raced through the dark, rain-swollen streets. Although time was of the essence, I did double back once to be on the safe side. Finally, I hailed a "gypsy cab" to haul me to within a couple blocks of my destination.

In my line of business, I have resources that work both sides of the street. That night, I had to cash in numerous markets from the "dark side." I had made contact with them right before my lockdown and explained my situation. I hoped they would respond in kind.

Out of the rain at last, I changed into my dry clothes (my rain coat was of no use). After a cup or two of hot coffee, my contacts whisked me away across the river and into New Jersey.

Around 1:00am, we arrived at a cluster of seemingly abandoned warehouses situated on an older section of the New Jersey docks.

We entered through a darkened hallway of a small, four-story warehouse and into a large, open bay blazing with lights.

My benefactors were preparing to load an old "U-Haul" van with the goods I requested. But first, I needed to look over the inventory as they loaded the van.

Along with the van, I received more IDs and legal and insurance papers pertaining to the van. The van was also equipped with a small, but powerful, police radio, hidden in the small storage space (the van was part of the side business owned by my "friends"). Other items included money (old bills of small denominations) and maps showing safe back roads and places to stay throughout the surrounding states. I was offered a choice of weapons, but to be apprehended with one; my future would end right there.

The best "weapon" I received came from the last item on the list, "a detailed report of the location of my quarry."

Finally, the time to depart was at hand. My resource's debt to me had been paid in full. Time to sever all contact and ties. Most of the group had already departed, retreating back to the various haunts of the "nether world."

I drove out of the darkened warehouse, wondering what other obstacles would lie across "the path of my destiny."

Finally, my story is up-to-date. The last three days were spent travelling the back roads of several states. Now, I am tooling down route A1A along Florida's east coast.

My destination is a small, out-of-the-way town a few miles north of West Palm Beach. Hopefully, I will be able to apprehend the agent before he slips out of the country.

The big question is why is he still here? His ex-bosses would have agents and other local assets tracking him down. He probably needs an opportunity by something or someone to give them the slip.

As for the police radio, no news of my escape, just local traffic as I travelled through the various states. Although, on the regular broadcast, I heard of some reconstruction and renovation of warehouses along the New Jersey docks. My ex-resources know how to cover their tracks.

The warm sun and ocean breeze on my face is like nectar handed down from the gods, washing away all the anguish from the last few days. My mind is wandering, thinking of my life as one big "X." Ex-wife, no offspring, no close relatives, and a few missed opportunities...

"Adrian," I say to myself, "concentrate on the job ahead."

Suddenly, a large, nondescript object hits the white surface with a loud *bam* and an uproar from above.

The yellow pole breaks into numerous splinters, sending black marks and dust over the surface.

Adrian is now confused from the loud noise of the jumbled words and thoughts going through his mind. Everything is swirling like water going down a drain. To make matters worse, the warm sun and ocean breeze is replaced by the same grayish void that Adrian started from.

Standing on the white surface, the panic-stricken Adrian, with anguished eyes, looks and waits for the large, red object from above. But this time, nothing. Instead, the white surface starts bending from all sides, along with a sound like grunts and groans.

The light is fading as the sides are bending over each other, tighter and tighter.

Adrian can't see or breathe as the sides completely engulf him. Now it is a crumbled, white sphere, which in turn is tossed into a round, metal container and into oblivion.

Is this the end of Adrian?

Only time will tell.

CONDUCTOR: Magic

Dawn E. Dagger

LIGHTNING,
Sparking from fingertips.
The room
Tastes of metal
And anticipation.

Pages flutter
In unseen breezes.
Music,
Bending to each
Flick of the wrist—
To each
Delicate twitch

Of the wand.

The strings vibrate,
The woodwinds hum,
Each instrument awaiting
Its turn
To tremble and thrash
To dance and wail
To produce fine music
And vivid images
And emotions.

Rising
Swelling
Like the waves
Like the bass.

A crescendo,
A crescendo!

Decrescendo...
Quieter now.

The third act is done.
Sweat slicks brows;

Glistening diamonds
On inked papers
And foreheads.

Was it music?
Was it a story?
Perhaps it was magic.

Looking at the trembling air,
The wand of precise control,
The effort,
And the passion,
The answer becomes clear:
It is indeed
Magic.

About the Authors

Alexxa Burton

Alexxa has spent most of her life in Ohio when she wasn't busy exploring the planet Miaca. She has also released *From Winter* and several children's books.

When she's not writing, she spends her time in the kitchen creating masterpieces of a different type or spending time with her dogs and cat.

Barbara Lang

Barbara lives on a farm with cats (many of which are adoptable and have been altered), chickens, dogs, and cattle in Holmes County. For thirty wonderful years, she had the best job in the world working as a sales representative in the library market. A graduate of University of Akron and Kent State University, she also took courses at University of Michigan when she lived near Ann Arbor for 12 years.

Currently she is working on her second novel and owns an Airbnb between Millersburg and Loudonville.

Bill Reid

William E. Reid retired from Goodyear Aerospace in 1991 as a tool designer. From 1994-2007 he was a part of the Football Hall of Fame Festival Communications Committee. From 1984-2011 he was the Assistant Chair for the V.I.P Transportation of the Firestone Country Club Gold Tournament. He sold five photographs for the "Relay for Life" at the Massillon Museum, and had some of his photography printed in the Akron Life and Leisure magazine in 2003.

Bill started writing stories in 2018, and 'kicked them around' for a while. They laid dormant for about a year, and after many rewrites, finished them at the end of 2022/beginning of 2023.

Oblivion!! appeared in a book of which there is only one copy, belonging to Bill, titled "Grandpa Bill's Wonderful Stories Volume 1."

Cat Russell

Cat Russell lives in Ohio, with her high school sweetheart and their son, while writing and learning more about the craft every day. Her work has been published in print and online, and she is the author of several books of poetry and prose: *Soul Picked Clean* (March 2019), *An Optimist's Journal of the End of Days and Other Stories* (August 2020), *Pinholes: Traveling through the Curtain of the Night* (November 2021), *Kaleidoscope*, (September 2022), and her first self-published book, *Braving Persephone's Chill: Broken Haiku* (February 2024). She blogs monthly, podcasts occasionally, and is often mildly serious except when she's not.

When not writing or drinking copious quantities of tea, she can be found online at Twitter (@PoetCatRussell), Facebook (@ganymeder), or Instagram (@authorcatrussell). For more of her work, check out her writing blog (www.catrussellwriter.wordpress.com) and her Patreon page (www.patreon.org/authorcatrussell).

Dawn E. Dagger

An avid reader and writer for as long as she can remember, Dawn Dagger is a free–spirited author who loves everything fantastical and caffeinated.

Dawn lives in Ohio, where she works as the marketing specialist for her local library. She enjoys adventuring with her husband, friends, and two cats.

She makes art at every opportunity she can. Whether cross-stitching, designing websites, making commentary and gaming YouTube videos, teaching herself the piano, or something entirely new, she's always busy.

For more information or to connect with her, find Dawn and all of her books at:

Linktr.ee/dawndagger

Donna J. Bunner

Donna grew up in Norton, Ohio. Upon graduation, she received two associate degrees, one in Executive Secretary and the other in Medical Secretary from the University of Akron. Donna developed a love for the special needs community after attending her daughter's classroom activities in the multihandicapped classroom. Donna has held several hats during her life from being a single parent to being a medical transcriptionist. She has also served in Special Needs Ministries in Stark County.

Today Donna works as a Direct Support Professional serving the Special Needs Community.

Donna enjoys needlepoint with plastic canvas, researching family history, spending time with family, friends, and cats, scrapbooking, Vera Bradley purses, reading Holocaust stories especially *The Diary of Anne Frank*, and attending church. Donna is also part of the Massillon Public Library Adult Writing Group as she hopes to create writings about her faith and autism.

Dwight Parrish

Dwight Parrish is a retired customer relations supervisor who always had a passion for writing. He holds a Bachelor's Degree in Finance and a Master's Degree in Business Administration.

In the early stages of retirement, he completed a creative writing course at Malone University.

He enjoys reading, hanging out at the beach, and listening to music. Dwight and his wife Cyndie live in Northeast Ohio. They have (3) children, (7) grandchildren, and (1) great- grandson.

His debut poetry collection, *Sketches of Me*, and his memoir, *In My Father's House*, are bestsellers.

John Echols

John Echols is an avid sports fan who mainly writes books on his favorite topics. He loves all sports, with the possible exception of swimming. He lives in Ohio, incidentally, not far from the NFL Hall of Fame.

LML McClure

LML McClure was inspired to write out her thoughts after reading the book written by a university friend. She shared her journaling with other aspiring and published authors in the Writers of the Round Table group, and she has greatly appreciated the encouragement and guidance of the members.

LML is a retired teacher and administrative assistant. She hopes to pull from past sorrows and joys and create from them prose or poetry that may inspire others.

www.ingramcontent.com/pod-product-compliance
Lightning Source LLC
La Vergne TN
LVHW050934080826
845145LV00004B/1262

9781968575137